Gigi & Jacques
Claudette & Philippe
Request the honor
of your presence
at their

Wedding in Paris

Please join us in
Le Parc

Reception
to follow

Please
R.S.V.P.
_____
Your Name

Gigi & Jacques' Wedding in Paris

written & illustrated by

Maureen Edgecomb

PUBLISHED EXCLUSIVELY

for

CE Inc.

Published in the United States 2010
by Ravenwood Studios
PO. Box 197
Diamond Springs, California 95619

Exclusively for
CE Inc.

Gigi Paris and Jacques are trademarks of CE, Inc.

Book Design by Ruth Marcus, Sequim, WA

First Edition

ISBN # 978-0-9718604-5-2

Printed in China / January 2010

To order more books phone: 800-843-1043

Gigi and Jacques and Claudette and Philippe
loved to go to the park in Paris where they first met.

Jacques especially loved visiting his friends there.

Philippe and Claudette enjoyed these visits, too.
"Today we go straight to the top," Philippe said.
"To the top?" asked Claudette
"Oui," Philippe answered, "to the top of the Eiffel Tower.
Today is a special day!"

So, they went way up to the top of the Eiffel Tower where they could see the whole city of Paris below. Philippe took Claudette's hand and asked, "Claudette, will you marry me?"
"Oui, but of course!" Claudette answered.

When Jacques heard these words, he couldn't wait to ask Gigi!
He took her paw in his and asked, "Gigi, ma cheri, will you marry me?"
Blushing, Gigi sighed, "Oui, but of course, my own Jacques!"

So, they began to make plans.
Where would they get married?

Notre-Dame?

The Eiffel Tower?

Sacré-Coeur?

Le Parc?
Yes, Yes, oui! But of course!
The park where we met!

They were so excited that
Claudette and Philippe waved
their arms in joy!
Gigi danced,
and Jacques chased his tail!

Later that night . . .

they all dreamed
of their wedding day.

But the next day,
they had second
thoughts.

Claudette asked Gigi,
"Do you suppose we will have
to pick up after them?"

Philippe asked Jacques,
"Do you suppose pink might
be a color in our art studio?
Oh, but she will be
so beautiful…"

So, the preparations began.
Claudette addressed the invitations . . .

and Philippe told everyone.

Gigi and Claudette picked out the perfect gown.

Philippe and Jacques picked out the rings
and other important jewelry.

Finally, the wedding day came!
But they were all so much in love, they couldn't think straight!

Gigi gazed in the
mirror too long.

Claudette lost track of time.

Philippe forgot where
he put the rings.

And Jacques could only
dream of Gigi.

They hurried out their doors . . .

and as fast as they could . . .

they searched all over Paris!

They were late for their own wedding
and couldn't remember where to go!

Was the wedding at the
Arc de Triomphe?

The Moulin Rouge?

The fun park?

Should they take the train to Provence?

Should they go to Notre-Dame?

Sacré-Coeur?

The Eiffel Tower?

Oh, yes, but of course, Le Parc!

When they finally arrived, the guests were already waiting.

So, the wedding began, and as the music played…

first came oscar, the ring bearer . . .

then came Cookie, the flower girl . . .

followed by all the
beautiful bridesmaids.

Trés belle !

Philippe, Jacques and
the groomsmen all
waited at the altar.

Just then, the crowd hushed.
As the music played, everyone stood as
Gigi and Claudette walked down the aisle.
They were so very beautiful.

Gigi could only see Jacques.

And Jacques could only see Gigi.

Claudette said,
"But of course, I do."

Philippe said,
"Absolutely, I do."

Gigi sniffled, "Oui, I do."
And Jacques sighed, "Forever, I do!"

And then they danced . . .

But there were other cakes
and favors for all the guests.

Claudette and Gigi
tossed their bouquets.

Philippe gave Claudette a gift . . .

Claudette gave Philippe a gift . . .

Mon Amour !

and Gigi and Jacques
exchanged gifts, too.

BISCUITS

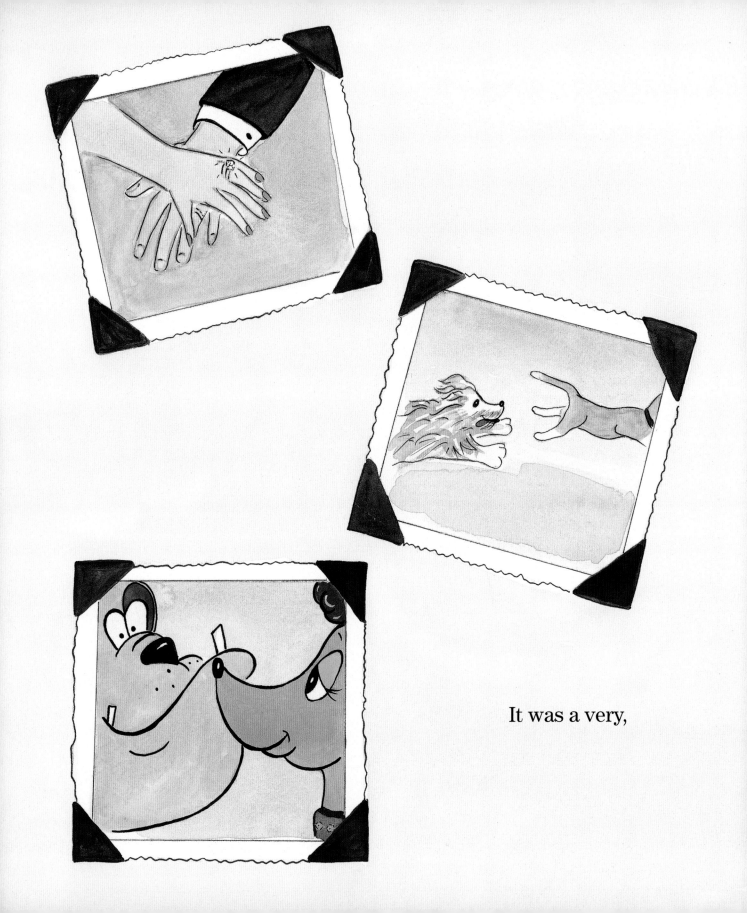

It was a very,

very special day . . .

Mes félicitations!

that became a wonderful,
special night in the very
heart of Paris.

Merci Beaucoup

Thank You
for
coming to our
Wedding!

Au Revoir

Gigi & Jacques

Claudette & Philippe